The Prince and the Pa

Mark Twain

Alpha Editions

This edition published in 2024

ISBN 9789362099723

Design and Setting By

Alpha Editions

www.alphaedis.com

Email - info@alphaedis.com

As per information held with us this book is in Public Domain.
This book is a reproduction of an important historical work.
Alpha Editions uses the best technology to reproduce historical work
in the same manner it was first published to preserve its original nature.
Any marks or number seen are left intentionally to preserve.

Contents

Chapter VIII. The question of the Seal. .... - 1 -

Chapter IX. The river pageant. .... - 4 -

Chapter X. The Prince in the toils. .... - 8 -

Chapter XI. At Guildhall. .... - 20 -

Chapter VIII. The question of the Seal.

About five o'clock Henry VIII. awoke out of an unrefreshing nap, and muttered to himself, "Troublous dreams, troublous dreams! Mine end is now at hand: so say these warnings, and my failing pulses do confirm it." Presently a wicked light flamed up in his eye, and he muttered, "Yet will not I die till HE go before."

His attendants perceiving that he was awake, one of them asked his pleasure concerning the Lord Chancellor, who was waiting without.

"Admit him, admit him!" exclaimed the King eagerly.

The Lord Chancellor entered, and knelt by the King's couch, saying—

"I have given order, and, according to the King's command, the peers of the realm, in their robes, do now stand at the bar of the House, where, having confirmed the Duke of Norfolk's doom, they humbly wait his majesty's further pleasure in the matter."

The King's face lit up with a fierce joy. Said he—

"Lift me up! In mine own person will I go before my Parliament, and with mine own hand will I seal the warrant that rids me of—"

His voice failed; an ashen pallor swept the flush from his cheeks; and the attendants eased him back upon his pillows, and hurriedly assisted him with restoratives. Presently he said sorrowfully—

"Alack, how have I longed for this sweet hour! and lo, too late it cometh, and I am robbed of this so coveted chance. But speed ye, speed ye! let others do this happy office sith 'tis denied to me. I put my Great Seal in commission: choose thou the lords that shall compose it, and get ye to your work. Speed ye, man! Before the sun shall rise and set again, bring me his head that I may see it."

"According to the King's command, so shall it be. Will't please your majesty to order that the Seal be now restored to me, so that I may forth upon the business?"

"THE ATTENDANTS EASED HIM BACK UPON HIS PILLOWS."

"The Seal? Who keepeth the Seal but thou?"

"Please your majesty, you did take it from me two days since, saying it should no more do its office till your own royal hand should use it upon the Duke of Norfolk's warrant."

"Why, so in sooth I did: I do remember . . . What did I with it? . . . I am very feeble . . . So oft these days doth my memory play the traitor with me . . . 'Tis strange, strange—"

The King dropped into inarticulate mumblings, shaking his grey head weakly from time to time, and gropingly trying to recollect what he had done with the Seal. At last my Lord Hertford ventured to kneel and offer information—

"Sire, if that I may be so bold, here be several that do remember with me how that you gave the Great Seal into the hands of his highness the Prince of Wales to keep against the day that—"

"True, most true!" interrupted the King. "Fetch it! Go: time flieth!"

Lord Hertford flew to Tom, but returned to the King before very long, troubled and empty-handed. He delivered himself to this effect—

"It grieveth me, my lord the King, to bear so heavy and unwelcome tidings; but it is the will of God that the prince's affliction abideth still, and he cannot recall to mind that he received the Seal. So came I quickly to report, thinking it were waste of precious time, and little worth withal, that any should attempt to search the long array of chambers and saloons that belong unto his royal high—"

A groan from the King interrupted the lord at this point. After a little while his majesty said, with a deep sadness in his tone—

"Trouble him no more, poor child. The hand of God lieth heavy upon him, and my heart goeth out in loving compassion for him, and sorrow that I may not bear his burden on mine old trouble-weighted shoulders, and so bring him peace."

He closed his eyes, fell to mumbling, and presently was silent. After a time he opened his eyes again, and gazed vacantly around until his glance rested upon the kneeling Lord Chancellor. Instantly his face flushed with wrath—

"What, thou here yet! By the glory of God, an' thou gettest not about that traitor's business, thy mitre shall have holiday the morrow for lack of a head to grace withal!"

The trembling Chancellor answered—

"Good your Majesty, I cry you mercy! I but waited for the Seal."

"Man, hast lost thy wits? The small Seal which aforetime I was wont to take with me abroad lieth in my treasury. And, since the Great Seal hath flown away, shall not it suffice? Hast lost thy wits? Begone! And hark ye—come no more till thou do bring his head."

The poor Chancellor was not long in removing himself from this dangerous vicinity; nor did the commission waste time in giving the royal assent to the work of the slavish Parliament, and appointing the morrow for the beheading of the premier peer of England, the luckless Duke of Norfolk.

Chapter IX. The river pageant.

At nine in the evening the whole vast river-front of the palace was blazing with light. The river itself, as far as the eye could reach citywards, was so thickly covered with watermen's boats and with pleasure-barges, all fringed with coloured lanterns, and gently agitated by the waves, that it resembled a glowing and limitless garden of flowers stirred to soft motion by summer winds. The grand terrace of stone steps leading down to the water, spacious enough to mass the army of a German principality upon, was a picture to see, with its ranks of royal halberdiers in polished armour, and its troops of brilliantly costumed servitors flitting up and down, and to and fro, in the hurry of preparation.

Presently a command was given, and immediately all living creatures vanished from the steps. Now the air was heavy with the hush of suspense and expectancy. As far as one's vision could carry, he might see the myriads of people in the boats rise up, and shade their eyes from the glare of lanterns and torches, and gaze toward the palace.

A file of forty or fifty state barges drew up to the steps. They were richly gilt, and their lofty prows and sterns were elaborately carved. Some of them were decorated with banners and streamers; some with cloth-of-gold and arras embroidered with coats-of-arms; others with silken flags that had numberless little silver bells fastened to them, which shook out tiny showers of joyous music whenever the breezes fluttered them; others of yet higher pretensions, since they belonged to nobles in the prince's immediate service, had their sides picturesquely fenced with shields gorgeously emblazoned with armorial bearings. Each state barge was towed by a tender. Besides the rowers, these tenders carried each a number of men-at-arms in glossy helmet and breastplate, and a company of musicians.

"A TROOP OF HALBERDIERS APPEARED IN THE GATEWAY."

breezes fluttered them; others of yet higher pretensions, since they belonged to nobles in the prince's immediate service, had their sides picturesquely fenced with shields gorgeously emblazoned with armorial bearings. Each state barge was towed by a tender. Besides the rowers, these tenders carried each a number of men-at-arms in glossy helmet and breastplate, and a company of musicians.

The advance-guard of the expected procession now appeared in the great gateway.

The advance-guard of the expected procession now appeared in the great gateway, a troop of halberdiers. They were dressed in striped hose of black and tawny, velvet caps graced at the sides with silver roses, and doublets of murrey and blue cloth, embroidered on the front and back with the three feathers, the prince's blazon, woven in gold. Their halberd staves were covered with crimson velvet, fastened with gilt nails, and ornamented with gold tassels. Filing off on the right and left, they formed two long lines, extending from the gateway of the palace to the water's edge. A thick rayed cloth or carpet was then unfolded, and laid down between them by attendants in the gold-and-crimson liveries of the prince. This done, a flourish of trumpets resounded from within. A lively prelude arose from the musicians on the water; and two ushers with white wands marched with a slow and stately pace from the portal. They were followed by an officer bearing the civic mace, after whom came another carrying the city's sword; then several sergeants of the city guard, in their full accoutrements, and with badges on their sleeves; then the Garter King-at-arms, in his tabard;

then several Knights of the Bath, each with a white lace on his sleeve; then their esquires; then the judges, in their robes of scarlet and coifs; then the Lord High Chancellor of England, in a robe of scarlet, open before, and purfled with minever; then a deputation of aldermen, in their scarlet cloaks; and then the heads of the different civic companies, in their robes of state. Now came twelve French gentlemen, in splendid habiliments, consisting of pourpoints of white damask barred with gold, short mantles of crimson velvet lined with violet taffeta, and carnation coloured hauts-de-chausses, and took their way down the steps. They were of the suite of the French ambassador, and were followed by twelve cavaliers of the suite of the Spanish ambassador, clothed in black velvet, unrelieved by any ornament. Following these came several great English nobles with their attendants.'

There was a flourish of trumpets within; and the Prince's uncle, the future great Duke of Somerset, emerged from the gateway, arrayed in a 'doublet of black cloth-of-gold, and a cloak of crimson satin flowered with gold, and ribanded with nets of silver.' He turned, doffed his plumed cap, bent his body in a low reverence, and began to step backward, bowing at each step. A prolonged trumpet-blast followed, and a proclamation, "Way for the high and mighty the Lord Edward, Prince of Wales!" High aloft on the palace walls a long line of red tongues of flame leapt forth with a thunder-crash; the massed world on the river burst into a mighty roar of welcome; and Tom Canty, the cause and hero of it all, stepped into view and slightly bowed his princely head.

"TOM CANTY STEPPED INTO VIEW."

He was 'magnificently habited in a doublet of white satin, with a frontpiece of purple cloth-of-tissue, powdered with diamonds, and edged with ermine. Over this he wore a mantle of white cloth-of-gold, pounced with the triple-feathered crest, lined with blue satin, set with pearls and precious stones, and fastened with a clasp of brilliants. About his neck hung the order of the Garter, and several princely foreign orders;' and wherever light fell upon him jewels responded with a blinding flash. O Tom Canty, born in a hovel, bred in the gutters of London, familiar with rags and dirt and misery, what a spectacle is this!

Chapter X. The Prince in the toils.

We left John Canty dragging the rightful prince into Offal Court, with a noisy and delighted mob at his heels. There was but one person in it who offered a pleading word for the captive, and he was not heeded; he was hardly even heard, so great was the turmoil. The Prince continued to struggle for freedom, and to rage against the treatment he was suffering, until John Canty lost what little patience was left in him, and raised his oaken cudgel in a sudden fury over the Prince's head. The single pleader for the lad sprang to stop the man's arm, and the blow descended upon his own wrist. Canty roared out—

"Thou'lt meddle, wilt thou? Then have thy reward."

"A DIM FORM SANK TO THE GROUND."

His cudgel crashed down upon the meddler's head: there was a groan, a dim form sank to the ground among the feet of the crowd, and the next moment it lay there in the dark alone. The mob pressed on, their enjoyment nothing disturbed by this episode.

Presently the Prince found himself in John Canty's abode, with the door closed against the outsiders. By the vague light of a tallow candle which was thrust into a bottle, he made out the main features of the loathsome den, and also the occupants of it. Two frowsy girls and a middle-aged woman cowered against the wall in one corner, with the aspect of animals habituated to harsh usage, and expecting and dreading it now. From another corner stole a withered hag with streaming grey hair and malignant eyes. John Canty said to this one—

"Tarry! There's fine mummeries here. Mar them not till thou'st enjoyed them: then let thy hand be heavy as thou wilt. Stand forth, lad. Now say thy foolery again, an thou'st not forgot it. Name thy name. Who art thou?"

The insulted blood mounted to the little prince's cheek once more, and he lifted a steady and indignant gaze to the man's face and said—

"'Tis but ill-breeding in such as thou to command me to speak. I tell thee now, as I told thee before, I am Edward, Prince of Wales, and none other."

THE PRINCE IN THE TOILS.

"WHO ART THOU?"

"O poor Tom, poor lad!"

The mother fell on her knees before the prince, put her hands upon his shoulders, and gazed yearningly into his face through her rising tears. Then she said,—

The stunning surprise of this reply nailed the hag's feet to the floor where she stood, and almost took her breath. She stared at the Prince in stupid amazement, which so amused her ruffianly son, that he burst into a roar of laughter. But the effect upon Tom Canty's mother and sisters was different. Their dread of bodily injury gave way at once to distress of a different sort. They ran forward with woe and dismay in their faces, exclaiming—

"Oh, poor Tom, poor lad!"

The mother fell on her knees before the Prince, put her hands upon his shoulders, and gazed yearningly into his face through her rising tears. Then she said—

"Oh, my poor boy! Thy foolish reading hath wrought its woeful work at last, and ta'en thy wit away. Ah! why did'st thou cleave to it when I so warned thee 'gainst it? Thou'st broke thy mother's heart."

The Prince looked into her face, and said gently—

"Thy son is well, and hath not lost his wits, good dame. Comfort thee: let me to the palace where he is, and straightway will the King my father restore him to thee."

"The King thy father! Oh, my child! unsay these words that be freighted with death for thee, and ruin for all that be near to thee. Shake of this gruesome dream. Call back thy poor wandering memory. Look upon me. Am not I thy mother that bore thee, and loveth thee?"

The Prince shook his head and reluctantly said—

"God knoweth I am loth to grieve thy heart; but truly have I never looked upon thy face before."

The woman sank back to a sitting posture on the floor, and, covering her eyes with her hands, gave way to heart-broken sobs and wailings.

"Let the show go on!" shouted Canty. "What, Nan!—what, Bet! mannerless wenches! will ye stand in the Prince's presence? Upon your knees, ye pauper scum, and do him reverence!"

He followed this with another horse-laugh. The girls began to plead timidly for their brother; and Nan said—

"An thou wilt but let him to bed, father, rest and sleep will heal his madness: prithee, do."

"Do, father," said Bet; "he is more worn than is his wont. To-morrow will he be himself again, and will beg with diligence, and come not empty home again."

This remark sobered the father's joviality, and brought his mind to business. He turned angrily upon the Prince, and said—

"The morrow must we pay two pennies to him that owns this hole; two pennies, mark ye—all this money for a half-year's rent, else out of this we go. Show what thou'st gathered with thy lazy begging."

The Prince said—

"Offend me not with thy sordid matters. I tell thee again I am the King's son."

A sounding blow upon the Prince's shoulder from Canty's broad palm sent him staggering into goodwife Canty's arms, who clasped him to her breast, and sheltered him from a pelting rain of cuffs and slaps by interposing her own person. The frightened girls retreated to their corner; but the grandmother stepped eagerly forward to assist her son. The Prince sprang away from Mrs. Canty, exclaiming—

"SENT HIM STAGGERING INTO GOODWIFE CANTY'S ARMS."

"Thou shalt not suffer for me, madam. Let these swine do their will upon me alone."

This speech infuriated the swine to such a degree that they set about their work without waste of time. Between them they belaboured the boy right soundly, and then gave the girls and their mother a beating for showing sympathy for the victim.

"Now," said Canty, "to bed, all of ye. The entertainment has tired me."

The light was put out, and the family retired. As soon as the snorings of the head of the house and his mother showed that they were asleep, the young girls crept to where the Prince lay, and covered him tenderly from the cold with straw and rags; and their mother crept to him also, and stroked his hair, and cried over him, whispering broken words of comfort and compassion in his ear the while. She had saved a morsel for him to eat, also; but the boy's pains had swept away all appetite—at least for black and tasteless crusts. He was touched by her brave and costly defence of him, and by her commiseration; and he thanked her in very noble and princely words, and begged her to go to her sleep and try to forget her sorrows. And he added that the King his father would not let her loyal kindness and devotion go unrewarded. This return to his 'madness' broke her heart anew, and she strained him to her breast again and again, and then went back, drowned in tears, to her bed.

As she lay thinking and mourning, the suggestion began to creep into her mind that there was an undefinable something about this boy that was lacking in Tom Canty, mad or sane. She could not describe it, she could not tell just what it was, and yet her sharp mother-instinct seemed to detect it and perceive it. What if the boy were really not her son, after all? Oh, absurd! She almost smiled at the idea, spite of her griefs and troubles. No matter, she found that it was an idea that would not 'down,' but persisted in haunting her. It pursued her, it harassed her, it clung to her, and refused to be put away or ignored. At last she perceived that there was not going to be any peace for her until she should devise a test that should prove, clearly and without question, whether this lad was her son or not, and so banish these wearing and worrying doubts. Ah, yes, this was plainly the right way out of the difficulty; therefore she set her wits to work at once to contrive that test. But it was an easier thing to propose than to accomplish. She turned over in her mind one promising test after another, but was obliged to relinquish them all—none of them were absolutely sure, absolutely perfect; and an imperfect one could not satisfy her. Evidently she was racking her head in vain—it seemed manifest that she must give the matter up. While this depressing thought was passing through her mind, her ear caught the regular breathing of the boy, and she knew he had fallen asleep. And while she listened, the measured breathing was broken by a soft, startled cry, such as one utters in a troubled dream. This chance occurrence furnished her instantly with a plan worth all her laboured tests combined. She at once set herself feverishly, but noiselessly, to work to relight her candle, muttering to herself, "Had I but seen him THEN, I should have known! Since that day, when he was little, that the powder burst in his face, he hath never been startled of a sudden out of his dreams or out of his thinkings, but he hath cast his hand before his eyes, even as he did that day; and not as others would do it, with the palm inward, but always with the palm turned outward—I have seen it a hundred times, and it hath never varied nor ever failed. Yes, I shall soon know, now!"

By this time she had crept to the slumbering boy's side, with the candle, shaded, in her hand. She bent heedfully and warily over him, scarcely breathing in her suppressed excitement, and suddenly flashed the light in his face and struck the floor by his ear with her knuckles. The sleeper's eyes sprang wide open, and he cast a startled stare about him—but he made no special movement with his hands.

"SHE BENT HEEDFULLY AND WARILY OVER HIM."

By this time she had crept to the slumbering boy's side, with the candle, shaded, in her hand. She bent heedfully and warily over him, scarcely breathing, in her suppressed excitement, and suddenly flashed the light in his face and struck the floor by his ear with her knuckles. The sleeper's eyes sprung wide open, and he cast a startled stare about him — but he made no special movement with his hands.

The poor woman was smitten almost helpless with surprise and grief; but she contrived to hide her emotions, and to soothe the boy to sleep again; then she crept apart and communed miserably with herself upon the disastrous result of her experiment. She tried to believe that her Tom's madness had banished this habitual gesture of his; but she could not do it. "No," she said, "his HANDS are not mad; they could not unlearn so old a habit in so brief a time. Oh, this is a heavy day for me!"

Still, hope was as stubborn now as doubt had been before; she could not bring herself to accept the verdict of the test; she must try the thing again—the failure must have been only an accident; so she startled the boy out of his sleep a second and a third time, at intervals—with the same result which had marked the first test; then she dragged herself to bed, and fell sorrowfully asleep, saying, "But I cannot give him up—oh no, I cannot, I cannot—he MUST be my boy!"

"THE PRINCE SPRANG UP."

The poor mother's interruptions having ceased, and the Prince's pains having gradually lost their power to disturb him, utter weariness at last sealed his eyes in a profound and restful sleep. Hour after hour slipped away, and still he slept like the dead. Thus four or five hours passed. Then his stupor began to lighten. Presently, while half asleep and half awake, he murmured—

"Sir William!"

After a moment—

"Ho, Sir William Herbert! Hie thee hither, and list to the strangest dream that ever . . . Sir William! dost hear? Man, I did think me changed to a pauper, and . . . Ho there! Guards! Sir William! What! is there no groom of the chamber in waiting? Alack! it shall go hard with—"

"What aileth thee?" asked a whisper near him. "Who art thou calling?"

"Sir William Herbert. Who art thou?"

"I? Who should I be, but thy sister Nan? Oh, Tom, I had forgot! Thou'rt mad yet—poor lad, thou'rt mad yet: would I had never woke to know it again! But prithee master thy tongue, lest we be all beaten till we die!"

The startled Prince sprang partly up, but a sharp reminder from his stiffened bruises brought him to himself, and he sank back among his foul straw with a moan and the ejaculation—

"Alas! it was no dream, then!"

In a moment all the heavy sorrow and misery which sleep had banished were upon him again, and he realised that he was no longer a petted prince in a palace, with the adoring eyes of a nation upon him, but a pauper, an outcast, clothed in rags, prisoner in a den fit only for beasts, and consorting with beggars and thieves.

In the midst of his grief he began to be conscious of hilarious noises and shoutings, apparently but a block or two away. The next moment there were several sharp raps at the door; John Canty ceased from snoring and said—

"Who knocketh? What wilt thou?"

A voice answered—

"Know'st thou who it was thou laid thy cudgel on?"

"No. Neither know I, nor care."

"Belike thou'lt change thy note eftsoons. An thou would save thy neck, nothing but flight may stead thee. The man is this moment delivering up the ghost. 'Tis the priest, Father Andrew!"

"God-a-mercy!" exclaimed Canty. He roused his family, and hoarsely commanded, "Up with ye all and fly—or bide where ye are and perish!"

Scarcely five minutes later the Canty household were in the street and flying for their lives. John Canty held the Prince by the wrist, and hurried him along the dark way, giving him this caution in a low voice—

"Mind thy tongue, thou mad fool, and speak not our name. I will choose me a new name, speedily, to throw the law's dogs off the scent. Mind thy tongue, I tell thee!"

"HURRIED HIM ALONG THE DARK WAY."

Scarcely five minutes later the Canty household were in the street and flying for their lives. John Canty held the prince by the wrist, and hurried him along the dark way, giving him this caution in a low voice—

"Mind thy tongue, thou mad fool, and speak not our name. I will choose me a new name, speedily, to throw the law's dogs off the scent. Mind thy tongue, I tell thee!"

He growled these words to the rest of the family—

"If it so chance that we be separated, let each make for London bridge; whoso findeth himself as far as the last linen-draper's shop on the bridge, let him tarry there till the others be come, then will we flee into Southwark together."

He growled these words to the rest of the family—

"If it so chance that we be separated, let each make for London Bridge; whoso findeth himself as far as the last linen-draper's shop on the bridge, let him tarry there till the others be come, then will we flee into Southwark together."

At this moment the party burst suddenly out of darkness into light; and not only into light, but into the midst of a multitude of singing, dancing, and shouting people, massed together on the river frontage. There was a line of bonfires stretching as far as one could see, up and down the Thames; London Bridge was illuminated; Southwark Bridge likewise; the entire river was aglow with the flash and sheen of coloured lights; and constant explosions of fireworks filled the skies with an intricate commingling of shooting splendours and a thick rain of dazzling sparks that almost turned night into day; everywhere were crowds of revellers; all London seemed to be at large.

John Canty delivered himself of a furious curse and commanded a retreat; but it was too late. He and his tribe were swallowed up in that swarming hive of humanity, and hopelessly separated from each other in an instant. We are not considering that the Prince was one of his tribe; Canty still kept his grip upon him. The Prince's heart was beating high with hopes of escape, now. A burly waterman, considerably exalted with liquor, found himself rudely shoved by Canty in his efforts to plough through the crowd; he laid his great hand on Canty's shoulder and said—

"Nay, whither so fast, friend? Dost canker thy soul with sordid business when all that be leal men and true make holiday?"

"Mine affairs are mine own, they concern thee not," answered Canty, roughly; "take away thy hand and let me pass."

"Sith that is thy humour, thou'lt NOT pass, till thou'st drunk to the Prince of Wales, I tell thee that," said the waterman, barring the way resolutely.

"Give me the cup, then, and make speed, make speed!"

Other revellers were interested by this time. They cried out—

"The loving-cup, the loving-cup! make the sour knave drink the loving-cup, else will we feed him to the fishes."

So a huge loving-cup was brought; the waterman, grasping it by one of its handles, and with the other hand bearing up the end of an imaginary napkin, presented it in due and ancient form to Canty, who had to grasp the opposite handle with one of his hands and take off the lid with the other, according to ancient custom. This left the Prince hand-free for a second, of course. He wasted no time, but dived among the forest of legs about him and disappeared. In another moment he could not have been harder to find, under that tossing sea of life, if its billows had been the Atlantic's and he a lost sixpence.

imaginary napkin, presented it in due and ancient form to Canty, who had to grasp the opposite handle with one of his hands and take off the lid with the other, according to ancient custom.¹ This left the prince hand-free for a second, of course. He wasted no time, but dived among the forest of legs about him and disappeared. In another moment he could not have been harder to find, under that tossing sea of life, if its billows had been the Atlantic's and he a lost sixpence.

"HE WASTED NO TIME."

He very soon realized this fact, and straightway busied himself about his own affairs without further thought of John Canty. He quickly realized another thing, too. To wit, that a spurious Prince of Wales was being feasted by the city in his stead. He easily concluded that the pauper lad, Tom Canty, had deliberately taken advantage of his stupendous opportunity and become a usurper.

He very soon realised this fact, and straightway busied himself about his own affairs without further thought of John Canty. He quickly realised another thing, too. To wit, that a spurious Prince of Wales was being feasted by the city in his stead. He easily concluded that the pauper lad, Tom Canty, had deliberately taken advantage of his stupendous opportunity and become a usurper.

Therefore there was but one course to pursue—find his way to the Guildhall, make himself known, and denounce the impostor. He also made up his mind that Tom should be allowed a reasonable time for spiritual preparation, and then be hanged, drawn and quartered, according to the law and usage of the day in cases of high treason.

Chapter XI. At Guildhall.

The royal barge, attended by its gorgeous fleet, took its stately way down the Thames through the wilderness of illuminated boats. The air was laden with music; the river banks were beruffled with joy-flames; the distant city lay in a soft luminous glow from its countless invisible bonfires; above it rose many a slender spire into the sky, incrusted with sparkling lights, wherefore in their remoteness they seemed like jewelled lances thrust aloft; as the fleet swept along, it was greeted from the banks with a continuous hoarse roar of cheers and the ceaseless flash and boom of artillery.

To Tom Canty, half buried in his silken cushions, these sounds and this spectacle were a wonder unspeakably sublime and astonishing. To his little friends at his side, the Princess Elizabeth and the Lady Jane Grey, they were nothing.

Arrived at the Dowgate, the fleet was towed up the limpid Walbrook (whose channel has now been for two centuries buried out of sight under acres of buildings) to Bucklersbury, past houses and under bridges populous with merry-makers and brilliantly lighted, and at last came to a halt in a basin where now is Barge Yard, in the centre of the ancient city of London. Tom disembarked, and he and his gallant procession crossed Cheapside and made a short march through the Old Jewry and Basinghall Street to the Guildhall.

Tom and his little ladies were received with due ceremony by the Lord Mayor and the Fathers of the City, in their gold chains and scarlet robes of state, and conducted to a rich canopy of state at the head of the great hall, preceded by heralds making proclamation, and by the Mace and the City Sword. The lords and ladies who were to attend upon Tom and his two small friends took their places behind their chairs.

scarlet robes of state, and conducted to a rich canopy of state at the head of the great hall, preceded by heralds making proclamation, and by the Mace and the City Sword. The lords and ladies who were to attend upon Tom and his two small friends took their places behind their chairs.

At a lower table the court grandees and other guests of noble degree were seated, with the magnates of the city; the commoners took places at a multitude of tables on the main floor of the hall. From their lofty vantage-ground, the giants Gog and Magog, the ancient guardians of the city, contemplated the spectacle below them with eyes

"A RICH CANOPY OF STATE."

grown familiar to it in forgotten generations. There was a bugle-blast and a proclamation, and a fat butler appeared in a high perch in the leftward wall, followed by his servitors bearing with impressive solemnity a royal Baron of Beef, smoking hot and ready for the knife.

At a lower table the Court grandees and other guests of noble degree were seated, with the magnates of the city; the commoners took places at a multitude of tables on the main floor of the hall. From their lofty vantage-ground the giants Gog and Magog, the ancient guardians of the city, contemplated the spectacle below them with eyes grown familiar to it in forgotten generations. There was a bugle-blast and a proclamation, and a fat butler appeared in a high perch in the leftward wall, followed by his servitors bearing with impressive solemnity a royal baron of beef, smoking hot and ready for the knife.

After grace, Tom (being instructed) rose—and the whole house with him—and drank from a portly golden loving-cup with the Princess Elizabeth; from her it passed to the Lady Jane, and then traversed the general assemblage. So the banquet began.

By midnight the revelry was at its height. Now came one of those picturesque spectacles so admired in that old day. A description of it is still extant in the quaint wording of a chronicler who witnessed it:

'Space being made, presently entered a baron and an earl appareled after the Turkish fashion in long robes of bawdkin powdered with gold; hats on their heads of crimson velvet, with great rolls of gold, girded with two swords, called scimitars, hanging by great bawdricks of gold. Next came yet another baron and another earl, in two long gowns of yellow satin, traversed with white satin, and in every bend of white was a bend of crimson satin, after the fashion of Russia, with furred hats of gray on their heads; either of them having an hatchet in their hands, and boots with pykes' (points a foot long), 'turned up. And after them came a knight, then the Lord High Admiral, and with him five nobles, in doublets of crimson velvet, voyded low on the back and before to the cannell-bone, laced on the breasts with chains of silver; and over that, short cloaks of crimson satin, and on their heads hats after the dancers' fashion, with pheasants' feathers in them. These were appareled after the fashion of Prussia. The torchbearers, which were about an hundred, were appareled in crimson satin and green, like Moors, their faces black. Next came in a mommarye. Then the minstrels, which were disguised, danced; and the lords and ladies did wildly dance also, that it was a pleasure to behold.'

And while Tom, in his high seat, was gazing upon this 'wild' dancing, lost in admiration of the dazzling commingling of kaleidoscopic colours which the whirling turmoil of gaudy figures below him presented, the ragged but real little Prince of Wales was proclaiming his rights and his wrongs, denouncing the impostor, and clamouring for admission at the gates of Guildhall! The crowd enjoyed this episode prodigiously, and pressed forward and craned their necks to see the small rioter. Presently they began to taunt him and mock at him, purposely to goad him into a higher and still more entertaining fury. Tears of mortification sprang to his eyes, but he stood his ground and defied the mob right royally. Other taunts followed, added mockings stung him, and he exclaimed—

"I tell ye again, you pack of unmannerly curs, I am the Prince of Wales! And all forlorn and friendless as I be, with none to give me word of grace or help me in my need, yet will not I be driven from my ground, but will maintain it!"

"Though thou be prince or no prince, 'tis all one, thou be'st a gallant lad, and not friendless neither! Here stand I by thy side to prove it; and mind I tell thee thou might'st have a worser friend than Miles Hendon and yet not tire thy legs with seeking. Rest thy small jaw, my child; I talk the language of these base kennel-rats like to a very native."

The speaker was a sort of Don Caesar de Bazan in dress, aspect, and bearing. He was tall, trim-built, muscular. His doublet and trunks were of rich material, but faded and threadbare, and their gold-lace adornments were sadly tarnished; his ruff was rumpled and damaged; the plume in his slouched hat was broken and had a bedraggled and disreputable look; at his side he wore a long rapier in a rusty iron sheath; his swaggering carriage marked him at once as a ruffler of the camp. The speech of this fantastic figure was received with an explosion of jeers and laughter. Some cried, "'Tis another prince in disguise!" "'Ware thy tongue, friend: belike he is dangerous!" "Marry, he looketh it—mark his eye!" "Pluck the lad from him—to the horse-pond wi' the cub!"

Instantly a hand was laid upon the Prince, under the impulse of this happy thought; as instantly the stranger's long sword was out and the meddler went to the earth under a sounding thump with the flat of it. The next moment a score of voices shouted, "Kill the dog! Kill him! Kill him!" and the mob closed in on the warrior, who backed himself against a wall and began to lay about him with his long weapon like a madman. His victims sprawled this way and that, but the mob-tide poured over their prostrate forms and dashed itself against the champion with undiminished fury.

"BEGAN TO LAY ABOUT HIM."

His moments seemed numbered, his destruction certain, when suddenly a trumpet-blast sounded, a voice shouted, "Way for the King's messenger!" and a troop of horsemen came charging down upon the mob, who fled out of harm's reach as fast as their legs could carry them. The bold stranger caught up the Prince in his arms, and was soon far away from danger and the multitude.

Return we within the Guildhall. Suddenly, high above the jubilant roar and thunder of the revel, broke the clear peal of a bugle-note. There was instant silence—a deep hush; then a single voice rose—that of the messenger from the palace—and began to pipe forth a proclamation, the whole multitude standing listening.

The closing words, solemnly pronounced, were—

"The King is dead!"

The great assemblage bent their heads upon their breasts with one accord; remained so, in profound silence, a few moments; then all sank upon their knees in a body, stretched out their hands toward Tom, and a mighty shout burst forth that seemed to shake the building—

"Long live the King!"

Return we within the Guildhall. Suddenly, high above the jubilant roar and thunder of the revel, broke the clear peal of a bugle-note. There was instant silence, — a deep hush; then a single voice rose — that of the messenger from the palace — and began to pipe forth a proclamation, the whole multitude standing, listening. The closing words, solemnly pronounced, were —

"The king is dead!"

The great assemblage

"LONG LIVE THE KING!"

Poor Tom's dazed eyes wandered abroad over this stupefying spectacle, and finally rested dreamily upon the kneeling princesses beside him, a moment, then upon the Earl of Hertford. A sudden purpose dawned in his face. He said, in a low tone, at Lord Hertford's ear—

"Answer me truly, on thy faith and honour! Uttered I here a command, the which none but a king might hold privilege and prerogative to utter, would such commandment be obeyed, and none rise up to say me nay?"

"None, my liege, in all these realms. In thy person hides the majesty of England. Thou art the king—thy word is law."

Tom responded, in a strong, earnest voice, and with great animation—

"Then shall the king's law be law of mercy, from this day, and never more be law of blood! Up from thy knees and away! To the Tower, and say the King decrees the Duke of Norfolk shall not die!"

The words were caught up and carried eagerly from lip to lip far and wide over the hall, and as Hertford hurried from the presence, another prodigious shout burst forth—

"The reign of blood is ended! Long live Edward, King of England!"